The AMAZING DAYS of ABBY HAYES

The Declaration of Independence

D0376324

Read all the books about me!

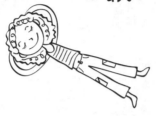

The Declaration of Independence

ANNE MAZER

AN
APPLE
PAPERBACK

SCHOLASTIC INC.
New York Toronto London Auckland Sydney
Mexico City New Delhi Hong Kong

Cover and interior illustrations
by Monica Gesue

Book design
by Dawn Adelman

No part of this publication may be reproduced in whole or in part, or stored in a retrieval system, or transmitted in any form or by any means, electronic, mechanical, photocopying, recording, or otherwise, without written permission of the publisher. For information regarding permission, write to Scholastic Inc., Attention: Permissions Department, 555 Broadway, New York, NY 10012.

ISBN 0-439-17876-2

12 11 10 9 8 7 6 5 4 3 2   0 1 2 3 4 5/0

Printed in the U.S.A   23

First Scholastic printing, August 2000

For Annika

Thanks to Jane for Web info,
to Max for tech support, and
to Mollie for enthusiasm and fifth-grade know-how.

The
AMAZING DAYS
of ABBY HAYES

The Declaration of Independence

Chapter 1

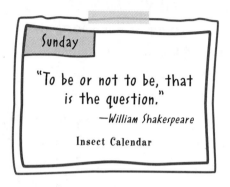

Sunday

"To be or not to be, that
is the question."
—William Shakespeare

Insect Calendar

To be __what__ is the question. And __why__ is another question. Why doesn't anyone ever ask that one?

Brianna is having a birthday party. She is inviting all the fifth-graders. It would be fun, except that we have to come in costume.

What shall I be? And why do I have to be anything but me?

When Abby Hayes joined her family in the living room, they were all in front of a blank television screen, while Alex, her seven-year-old brother, fiddled with the remote.

"Can you figure it out, Alex?" Eva demanded. Fresh from basketball practice, she paced up and down the living room, still in shorts and a jersey with number one emblazoned on the back.

Alex ignored her. Although he was only in second grade, he was a whiz in math and electronics; in his spare time, he put together computerized robots.

"Of course, he can figure it out!" Isabel, Eva's twin, exclaimed. She waved her fingernails, which she had just painted in five shades of violet, in the air. She was dressed in a long velvet skirt with matching Lycra top. There was a metal choker around her neck. "Alex knows what he's doing, don't you?"

"Mmmmph," Alex muttered. He pressed a button, and the screen turned blue, then went blank again.

"Abby, you got here just in time for the good part," her father joked, pointing to the empty screen. "I hope it's not too exciting for you."

Abby closed her eyes. "Tell me when the scary part is over!"

"Ha-ha, very funny," Eva said, doing jumping jacks in place.

Eva was the opposite of her twin in both style and personality. When she wasn't in sports clothes, she wore button-down shirts and neatly ironed jeans. And she never painted her nails.

On the couch, Abby's mother had spread out papers from her briefcase. Her reading glasses were perched on her nose. She had changed out of her tailored wool suit into sweatpants and a T-shirt.

"Mom, could you show up in court like that?" Abby asked. "In sweatpants and T-shirt?"

"Sure . . . of course." Her mother wasn't listening. She had to review a case before tomorrow morning. Sometimes Abby was tempted to write up her feelings in a legal brief and hand it to her mother just to get her undivided attention. But then she'd have to put a lot of "wherefores" and "thereuntos" and "hereunders" in her sentences, just like lawyers did.

Abby didn't want to write a lot of confusing words like that. Ms. Bunder, her favorite teacher, always said, "It's an art to write simple, clear sentences."

Maybe Ms. Bunder could do a creative writing class for lawyers, Abby thought. They needed one! She'd ask next time she saw her.

"Eva, will you stop that!" Isabel demanded as her sister jumped up and down, waving her arms and legs. "You look like a windmill."

"I'm increasing my respiration rate," Eva retorted. "The heart is a muscle. It needs to be exercised. You don't get exercise by painting your fingernails to match the wallpaper and sitting in the library all day."

"It's more important to exercise your mind!" Isabel shot back. "Mental concentration improves health and physical performance! You should know that, Eva. The best athletes work with the mind before the body."

"Oh, yeah?" Eva said.

Isabel was a champion debater, but that didn't stop Eva from arguing with her. She believed in the number one emblazoned on the back of her basketball jersey.

Abby sighed and sank down in her chair. She pulled out the purple journal that Ms. Bunder had given her the first day of creative writing class and opened it to a new page.

SuperSisters #1 and #2 are at it again. Mind versus matter. Or, as I read in my Genius Calendar, "What is matter? Never mind. What is mind? No matter." Ha-ha. That is a good quote. New friend Natalie bought me Genius Calendar last week. She moved here right before school started. She loves chemistry, mysteries, and Harry Potter books. (I wonder if there are other Potter heads in the fifth grade. I hope Natalie will not like them better than she likes me and Jessica.)

Decibel level of SuperSister argument has increased. Sonic boom about to happen. Father is ignoring screaming sisters. He is trying to help Alex get the VCR running again. Mother hears nothing. When roof

blows off house, she will be studying her brief. Concentration of mother is awesome. Now I know why she is a successful lawyer.

As for me, my journal is my best friend (aside from Jessica and maybe Natalie). Writing is a solace, as Ms. Bunder says.

I looked up "solace" in Isabel's dictionary. It sounded slippery, like cod liver oil, which is a disgusting medicine that kids have to take in

old-fashioned books. They all hate it!
Thank goodness we don't have cod liver oil
today. Solace means "alleviation of
distress or discomfort." It is like medicine,
but not nasty stuff like cod liver oil.

My journal is soothing and comforting like
a cozy pillow or music at night. It's like
my mother coming into my room when I'm
sick and putting her hand on my forehead.

It's . . . uh-oh! Interruption! We inter-
rupt this journal entry for an emergency an-
nouncement.

SuperSis Sonic Boom about to be heard.
Isabel's face turning color of purple fingernails. Eva huffing and puffing, but not from
exercise. Alex valiantly working to get VCR
on track before house blows apart from
force of sisters' galelike fury. Father smiling
and pretending nothing is happening. Mother
still reading brief. Is my journal sonic-boom
proof????

Eva and Isabel faced off, screaming insults. Abby
shut her journal and waited for the final explosion. It
was impossible to write with all this noise, anyway.

"Come on, Alex, do your magic," Abby urged.

Her little brother bent over the controls. As usual, his hair was standing up on his head, and his shirt was buttoned wrong. He wore one green sock and one blue one.

Her father always said, "Let them work it out themselves," but even though Isabel and Eva had had fourteen years to work it out, they still hadn't.

If the television got fixed, the twins might be distracted from their fight. Nothing less would do it. If Abby tried to step in between her warring sisters, they'd squash her.

Only her seven-year-old brother could save the day.

Alex pointed the remote at the screen. Light appeared, and then music began to play. A picture of pumpkins flashed on the screen.

"Hooray, Alex!" Abby yelled.

Eva and Isabel paused in their fight. Their mother looked up from her brief.

"The switch at the back was set on channel four, not three," Alex explained.

"What are we watching, anyway?" Abby asked.

"Last year's Harvest Festival at the high school."

It was a Hayes family tradition to help out with

the festival. Last year Eva manned the prize booth and Isabel dressed up like a fortune-teller. Abby's mother raffled cakes, and her father let kids throw wet sponges at his face.

Abby took Alex around to all the games and activities he wanted.

"Look, look!" Alex pointed to the screen. In the midst of crowds of excited children bobbing for apples and getting their faces painted, a spaceship appeared. It flew crazily through the room, bounced off the gymnasium walls, and then abruptly disappeared.

"I don't remember any UFO's at the festival," their father said.

"I did it with the computer!" Alex cried. "It was easy!"

"Very cute, Alex," Abby said.

Their mother nodded. "I should get you to edit the videotapes of our annual board meetings. They could use a spaceship or two."

"When's the festival this year?" their father asked.

"In a month." Eva got up from the couch.

"Are we all going?" their mother asked.

"Yes!" the twins chimed.

Their father smiled. "It's nice to hear you two agree for a change."

"Abby, you'll take Alex again, right?" her mother said.

Abby took a deep breath. She loved her younger brother, and they did many things together. They played chess (not a lot, because she always lost), Rollerbladed, biked, and baked cookies together. When she was training hard for the soccer team, Alex had helped her out, even though he didn't know much about soccer.

It wasn't that she didn't want to be with Alex anymore, it was just that she wanted to be with her friends more. Next year she would be in middle school. She was old enough to go out more on her own, to have more independence.

Besides, the festival would be so much fun if she could wander around with her friends! There were games of skill, music, cotton candy, cakes, prizes, and crowds of people having a good time.

"I want to go with my friends," she announced. "I want to bike to the festival by myself with Natalie and Jessica."

Chapter 2

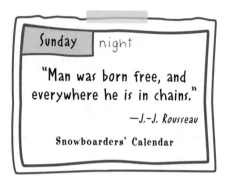

Sunday | night

"Man was born free, and
everywhere he is in chains."

—J.-J. Rousseau

Snowboarders' Calendar

Ha! That's for sure! I bet whoever wrote
this knew my family.

And now your roving reporter, Abby Hayes,
brings you the latest from the Hayes family.

News flash! A shocked silence
greeted young Abby Hayes's
Declaration of Independence in
the Hayes living room. The bold
fifth-grader announced to her
family that she would no longer
be the companion for Alex Hayes

during this year's Harvest Festival at the high school.

"Ten-year-olds have the right to the pursuit of liberty, happiness, and pierced ears," she declared. "They do not have to take their little brothers everywhere."

"I'm not little!" Alex Hayes interrupted furiously.

Ignoring this interruption, Abby Hayes demanded the right to ride her bicycle to the festival with her fellow fifth-graders, Jessica and Natalie. She said that she wanted to have her face painted with butterflies without a second-grader waiting to be taken to the science booth. She announced that she no longer wanted to have her parents and older sisters accompany her everywhere.

The older Hayeses reacted with stunned disbelief. Paul Hayes, Abby's father, who often supports her when no one else does, expressed outrage and dismay.

"We were counting on you," he said. "We volunteered our time because we thought you would watch Alex. Now what are we going to do?"

Eva Hayes, star athlete and constant muscle flexer, said, "Why can't you take Alex with you? He has a bike! He can ride with you and your friends!"

Her fraternal twin, Isabel Hayes, pointed to Alex Hayes, who was frowning in the corner. "Look at the poor kid! He's so upset! How can you disappoint him like this?"

Only Olivia Hayes, who sometimes does not understand her ten-year-old daughter, spoke with the voice of reason. "Abby wants more freedom. That's only natural. However, she has to prove that she has the maturity to handle it. She has to take more responsibility. Can you do that, Abby?"

"Yes!" cried the young revolutionary.

After some discussion, her father agreed that this was fair. Isabel and Eva Hayes had to agree to change their schedules so they could take Alex Hayes to the festival. (They were not happy.)

I hereby declare...

Alex was not happy, either. "Isabel won't like it when I want to throw balls," he complained. "Eva will get bored at the science exhibits."

Paul Hayes tried to reassure his son. "Go to the science exhibit with Isabel and throw balls with Eva."

"Abby has always taken me. I want Abby and no one else!"

"We'll still do special things together," Abby Hayes promised him. "Maybe we can Rollerblade together this weekend."

Alex Hayes turned away and did not reply.

Olivia Hayes hugged him and told him that his sister was growing up.

"Does that mean I can get my ears pierced?" Abby Hayes asked quickly.

Olivia Hayes laughed and said no, but good try.

The family meeting broke up. Isabel Hayes returned to her studies. Eva Hayes resumed her calisthenics. Olivia Hayes put her glasses back on and returned to her brief. Paul Hayes went into the kitchen to clean up. Abby Hayes took her journal upstairs to write this news flash, while Alex Hayes repeated that he wasn't going to the festival without Abby.

Chapter 3

Tuesday | morning

"It takes one a long time
to become young."

—*Picasso*

**Monuments of
Ancient Greece Calendar**

I wish it took a short time to become old! If I were older, I wouldn't have to prove that I'm mature enough to go to the festival with my friends.

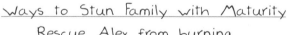

Ways to Stun Family with Maturity

Rescue Alex from burning building. (Must wait for burning building.)

Design Web page for Father's clients. (Must learn to use father's computer programs.)

Plead case for Mother in court. (Go to law school?)

Single-handedly save entire family from food poisoning. (Become doctor first. What if I have food poisoning, too? Forget about medical school. Call 911.)

These ideas too complicated and difficult. Must find something simpler but very impressive.

Think. Think. Think!

Make bed every morning.

Get own breakfast.

Put away clothes instead of leaving them on bed, chairs, desk, and floor.

(Aren't I supposed to do this stuff anyway?)

Don't whine when reminded to set table.

Don't say "Do I have to?" or "Why me?" when asked to sweep kitchen floor.

BRAINSTORM!!! Parents are always complaining about all the work they do and how they never get enough help around the house from their children, who are too busy with sports and school and friends.

Do extra chores that no one wants to do!!!

My parents will be awed, impressed, and bowled over by my maturity and responsibility. They will let me go to the festival AND Paradise Pizza by myself with Natalie and Jessica. Maybe they will even let me get my ears pierced!

Alex banged on Abby's door. "Jessica's here to pick you up for school!" he called.

Abby's best friend entered the room. Jessica was tall, especially next to Abby. She had straight shiny brown hair and large brown eyes. She was wearing her favorite outfit of overalls decorated with peace signs and smile buttons and a striped sweater underneath. An asthma inhaler peeked out from one of her overall pockets. Even though she had asthma, Jessica didn't let it stop her from becoming a very good athlete. She had helped Abby improve her soccer game at the beginning of soccer season.

"Coming in, Alex?" Abby called. Her brother often joined the girls for a few minutes in the morning.

"No!" He stomped off.

"What's with him?" Jessica asked.

"Alex?" Abby shrugged. "He's mad that I'm not taking him to the festival."

"Friends are important, too," Jessica said.

"Yes," Abby said. Too bad Alex wasn't as understanding as Jessica.

"I'll make it up to him, though," she promised. "We'll do something special and unforgettable together."

"What?"

"I don't know, but it'll be good!" Abby opened her bureau drawer. She couldn't think too much about her little brother right now. She had other things on her mind.

"Look," she said to Jessica, holding her gold hoop earrings to her ears. "Don't these look good?"

"Yes," Jessica agreed.

"My ears just cry out for earrings!" Abby exclaimed. "They look so plain and boring without them!"

"I know," Jessica sighed. She, too, had been campaigning to get her ears pierced. "I saw silver spaceship earrings in the mall." Abby's best friend loved anything to do with outer space. She planned to be an astronaut when she grew up. "My mother wouldn't let me buy them."

"I bet she'll get them for you for your birthday," Abby said. "Remember? That happened last year with the globe you wanted."

Jessica smiled. "You're right! Maybe she's planning to let me get my ears pierced for my birthday. Every time I mention earrings, she mysteriously changes the subject."

"My mother does, too," Abby said. "Mostly because she's sick of me talking about earrings all the time."

Jessica glanced around the room. "Almost ready to go?"

"Almost." Abby returned the hoops to their box in her drawer. She smoothed her hand over her curly red hair one last time — not that it did any good — and picked up her backpack.

"Wait! I almost forgot!" She dashed over to the bed, smoothed down the blankets, fluffed up the pillow, and pulled the comforter neatly over everything.

Her friend stared at her. "Abby! You're making your bed?"

Jessica was a neat freak. Her desk was neat, her room was neat, her homework was neat, and her mind was neat, too.

Abby was the opposite. Normally her room, her thoughts, and her pages were as messy and wild as her hair.

"I'm proving to my family how mature I am," Abby said. "Otherwise they won't let me go to the festival with you. Lucky you that you have such an easy mother!"

"You know what she's like."

"And you don't have younger brothers or sisters, either," Abby said enviously.

"Alex is great," Jessica said. "I'd take him any day."

The two girls went downstairs.

In the kitchen, Abby's father was reading the paper. As usual, he was in his bathrobe and unshaved. He had been up since early in the morning, working in his home office, setting up Web pages for his clients and advising them on how to do business on the Web.

Alex was upstairs packing his backpack for school.

The twins had left half an hour ago, and her mother had gone to the office early.

"Hi, Dad," Abby said. She took a bagel from the counter, smeared some cream cheese on it, and headed toward the door. "Bye, Dad."

"Breakfast, Abby?" Her father pointed to a chair. "Ever considered sitting down for it? Jessica? Hungry for some of my special French toast?"

"I already ate," Jessica said. "Thanks anyway."

"This is my breakfast, Dad." Abby waved the bagel in the air, hoping that her father wouldn't (a) lecture her on the importance of a healthy, relaxed start to the day; or (b) insist that she eat his special French toast. "We're going early to school to put up fall decorations."

"Pumpkins? Corn? Squash?"

"Colored crepe paper," Jessica explained. "And block prints that we made last week in art class."

"Ah. Well, have a good day in school, girls."

"Bye, Dad!" Abby picked up her backpack and headed for the door. "I'll be home late! We have soccer practice after school!"

She snatched her blue bucket hat from the closet.

"Good-bye, Alex!" she called.

There was no answer.

"GOOD-BYE, ALEX!" she yelled again.

Still nothing.

Abby exchanged a worried glance with Jessica. Sometimes Alex got mad, but not usually this mad.

"He'll get over it," Jessica said.

She hoped Jessica was right. She didn't have any siblings. Sometimes Abby envied her. Not having younger brothers or older sisters might be the secret of Jessica's calm. Abby sometimes wondered if Jessica got lonely without anyone to tease, torment, or play with at home.

She would offer to play chess with Alex tonight. That would put him in a better mood.

He had to get over it. He didn't have a choice. Abby refused to go to the festival with her family this year. She was ten years old. She had to make her stand sometime.

Chapter 4

Wednesday

"Happiness is contagious."

Old Sneakers Calendar

Is this true? Then why isn't my family dancing with joy that I want to go to the festival with my friends?

Brianna is happy about her birthday party. She didn't stop talking about it at soccer practice yesterday. A lot of other kids are happy, too—but not me!

I don't know what kind of costume to wear. It's too much to think about when I have to concentrate every ounce of my energy on proving how mature I am.

<u>Abby's Grown-up (Groan-up!) List</u>

Made bed for fourth day in a row. Even Isabel does not make her bed every day! Wonder how many bed makings it will take to set world record. (Check <u>Guinness Book of World Records</u>.)

Picked up muddy soccer clothes from bedroom floor and put them in hamper.

Threw crumpled math homework in trash instead of stuffing it in my backpack.

Cleared dishes without being nagged. (Mother had to ask me ONLY twice.)

Played chess with Alex. Did not accuse younger brother of cheating even after he won seven games in a row. Did not sweep chess pieces off board in frustration. Did not stomp off in a fury.

Incredible restraint and self-control.

I am mature; I am very mature. Why hasn't anyone in my family noticed????? They act as if everything is normal!

At school, everyone was talking about Brianna's party. Especially Brianna.

"I'm going to have a live band at my party," Brianna announced at lunchtime. "We're going to have dancing and refreshments. It'll be *the* party of the fifth grade."

She tossed her long dark hair over her shoulder and put her hand on her hip. She was wearing a glitter slip dress with matching suede platform shoes. Her arms were bare, but she wasn't shivering.

Sitting a few feet away with Natalie and Jessica, Abby shivered at the sight of Brianna. Was Brianna cold? Or just cold-blooded? How could she wear a sleeveless dress at the end of October! Maybe she needed a calendar to remind her what month it was.

There was an idea for a birthday present! She could buy Brianna a calendar with lots of places to put her own picture. Or would she prefer a brag book?

Abby took a bite of the egg-salad sandwich she had made for her lunch. It was way too salty. She had gotten distracted by an argument between her sisters as she was making it.

"Her cousins are in the band," Brianna's best friend Bethany said. "They're in middle school!"

Like her best friend, Bethany was dressed in a short dress and platform shoes. Her long blond hair was tied in a ponytail.

At least she wore a cardigan over the dress, Abby thought. Bethany imitated almost everything Brianna did, but she drew the line at wearing summer clothes in autumn.

"My cousins are professionals," Brianna emphasized. "They play at birthday parties and get paid for it."

"Probably toddlers' parties," Abby whispered to Jessica and Natalie.

Brianna glanced at Zach. "We're also going to give out prizes for the best costumes. Like Most Beautiful."

"That's Brianna," Bethany interrupted.

Brianna smiled graciously. "Or Funniest Costume or Most Original. I think you should try for Most Original, Zach. Weren't you a computer keyboard last year for Halloween?"

Zach ignored her. He was bent over the electronic game he had snuck into school.

Abby slid her journal onto her lap and picked up her purple pen.

What does Brianna see in Zach, any-way?

Hair: blond. Eyes: blue. Lashes: long and dark. A nose. A mouth. A chin. The usual stuff.

His mind: obsessed by electronics. (When Zach was a baby, he was found on a doorstep and raised by loving computers. A hard drive saved his life in his early years.)

He also likes soccer, ice hockey, and bas-ketball. His best friend is Tyler.

Conclusion: Zach looks and acts like every other fifth-grade boy.

Can't figure out why Brianna likes him. One of the great mysteries of the universe, like the pyramids or the Bermuda Triangle. Impossible to explain to a rational mind.

"What are you going to be for Brianna's party?" Jessica asked Natalie.

Abby took another bite of the salty egg-salad sand-wich, then washed it down with fruit juice. "I bet you're going to be Harry Potter."

"My parents don't want me to go." Natalie was thin, with short black hair. She didn't seem to care what she wore; her clothes were dark and rumpled. Sometimes they had stains on them from the chemistry experiments she performed.

"Why not?" Abby and Jessica demanded at the same time.

"I can't figure out what they think. I'm either too young or too old!" Natalie twirled her spoon in her yogurt cup. "If I were in first grade, it would be okay. If I were in ninth grade, it would be okay. But I'm a fifth-grader, so it's not okay. I'm stuck in the middle!"

"That stinks!" Abby cried.

"Maybe they'll change their minds about Brianna's party," Jessica said.

"Maybe," Natalie echoed doubtfully.

Abby wondered if she should ask her parents to call Natalie's parents. Could they talk them into letting her go? Her mother might plead Natalie's case. It was handy to have a lawyer in the family. Abby would ask her later.

"What about the festival?" Abby said. "Jessica and I were hoping that you would bike over with us. Will your parents let you?"

"I'll meet you at the festival," Natalie said. "My mother is going to sell tickets. I'll have to go with her."

Jessica stood up. "I'm going to get some chocolate milk. Either of you want anything?"

"An ice-cream bar." Abby rummaged in her pocket for change. She ought to be saving her allowance for the festival, not spending it on extra desserts. She was still hungry, though. Her sandwich was too awful to eat. She pushed it away.

"Are you going to throw that out?" Zach asked. "If you are, I'll take it."

"It's nasty," Abby warned him.

Zach bit into the sandwich. "It's good," he said. "I love egg salad."

Zach actually likes it!!! Do boys have some kind of garbage disposal in their stomachs? They will eat anything.

That sandwich is so salty that Zach will float if he finishes it.

Must concentrate when making lunch tomorrow.

Do not get near salt shaker unless calm and focused.

Or else buy school lunch.

No, would rather bring my own. That way I can prove my maturity to parents AND pack two desserts.

Costume idea #1: Mixed-up Costume. A black cat's tail (first grade) with a witch's mask (second grade) and a ghost sheet (third grade) and long red fingernails from my vampire costume (fourth grade). Ha-ha! I will win award for Most Confusing Costume!

I hope Brianna does not expect us to dance with the boys. She keeps looking at Zach every time she mentions dancing.

The bell rang. Abby closed her notebook, threw out her juice carton, and returned to the classroom with her friends.

Chapter 5

Saturday evening

"The cautious seldom err."
—Confucius

Salt and Pepper Shaker Calendar

The cautious seldom go to the Harvest Festival (or anywhere else) with their best friends.

Only the bold do what they want!

Asked Isabel the meaning of "err." (The word sounds like someone clearing their throat.) She said, "To make mistakes, like errors." I err all the time. But not about going to the festival with my friends!

<u>Abby's List of Bold Actions</u>
Continue to make bed, put dirty clothes in

hamper, throw out trash in wastebasket,
and clean up after myself.

   Clear table, even though it is Alex's week.
   Offer to make toast for father.
   Get mother's briefcase for work.
   Smile a lot. Even if my face hurts.

(Note: Checked <u>Guinness Book of World
Records</u>. There is no bed-making category.
Write letter to protest unfair policy. Or start
<u>Hayes Book of World Records</u> with cate-
gories for bed making, cheerful losing to
younger brothers, and longest unbroken record
for neat room kept by messy person.)

      <u>Family Reactions to Bold Actions</u>
   What they're supposed to say:
   "Abby, we can't believe you're only ten
years old! You're acting like an adult!
You're so mature and
responsible that we've decided
to let you have everything you
want. Of course, you can bike
to the festival with your friends,
and don't forget to stop off at

Paradise Pizza on your way home. Here's a twenty-dollar bill. Have fun spending it. Be sure to get home by evening, because we're going to the mall to get your ears pierced."

What they could have said:
"Great effort, Abby! You're well on your way to getting permission to go to the festival with your friends."

What they did say:
"Thanks, Abby. Could you find my glasses? I put them down somewhere."

Was hoping that Plan A (for Action) would Amaze and Awe my parents. Since it hasn't, must move on to Plan B (for Bigger, Better, and Bolder).

Only the most heroic actions will impress Paul and Olivia Hayes. I must be fearless, brave, strong. Will take on nastiest of chores without flinching. Will clean bathroom sink. I might even tackle the tub.

Change of Subject (Thank Goodness)

In our creative writing class on Thursday morning, Ms. Bunder talked to us about haiku. They are Japanese poems with three lines and seventeen syllables. A lot of haiku poems are about nature. We don't have to write exactly seventeen syllables — just three lines. She said to try to write something surprising in the last line.

Zach raised his hand and asked if the surprise could be winning a million dollars.

Ms. Bunder smiled and said yes, if it fits into the poem.

"I wrote haiku poems in summer camp," Brianna said. "My mother had them framed and gave them to all our friends."

Bethany raised her hand. "I got one, Ms. Bunder! It's about Brianna dancing."

Brianna said it would be hard to decide what to write about: her birthday party, dancing, or being soccer captain.

Jessica said she is going to write about looking at the planets.

Natalie is still deciding whether to write about Harry Potter again. She has already used him for the subject of six creative writing assignments. "Time to switch to chemistry poems," she said.

I wonder what I will write about.

Before Abby had a chance to write anything else, there was a knock at the door.

Eva entered Abby's bedroom. She sat down on the neatly made bed and gazed at the clean, vacuumed rug. Then she stared at the many calendars lining the walls, particularly Abby's favorite, the Spuds Calendar. She shook her head, sighed, then turned to her younger sister.

"Abby, will you do me a favor?"

Abby folded her arms. A tough, no-nonsense expression settled on her face. "What?" she demanded.

"I want to go to a hockey game tonight, but I have to clean the bathroom first."

"So?"

"I thought you could do it."

"Me? I don't clean bathrooms."

Abby wasn't going to let on that she had been planning to clean the bathroom that very night. She certainly wasn't going to reveal to her older sister that she had already taken a pair of rubber gloves and a sponge from the kitchen.

"Can't you do something for me?" Eva cried. "I'm bringing Alex to the festival while you run around with your friends!"

"Oh, right. Okay, I'll do it."

"Thanks, little sis. You're the best." Eva stood up to leave. "The cleaning stuff is under the sink," she reminded her. "Don't forget to polish the faucets!"

Note to self: A lucky break! Might have done Eva's work without knowing it. In future, make sure am not doing SuperSibs' chores when trying to prove maturity to parents!

Haiku Poems

1.

Wiping the bathroom sink
My hands wet with foaming cleanser.
Did someone coat the basin with
   dirt and mud?

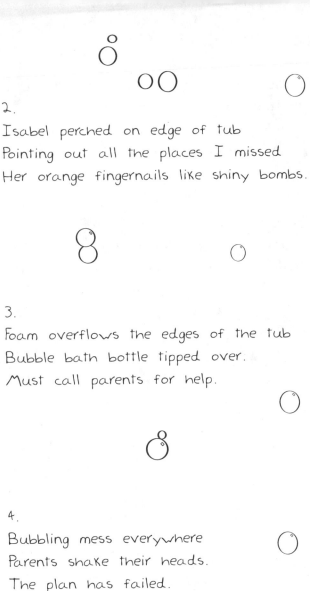

2.

Isabel perched on edge of tub
Pointing out all the places I missed
Her orange fingernails like shiny bombs.

3.

Foam overflows the edges of the tub
Bubble bath bottle tipped over.
Must call parents for help.

4.

Bubbling mess everywhere
Parents shake their heads.
The plan has failed.

Chapter 6

Why???

The world has too many questions and not enough answers!

My Parents' Questions

Why was the tub full of bubbles?

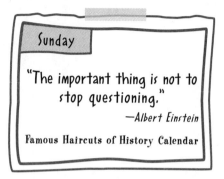

Why didn't I turn off the water before the bubbles started to go over the edge of the tub?

How come I used good towels to clean the mess up?

What was I doing in the bathroom, anyway? Wasn't it Eva's week to clean?

My Questions

Who forgot to tighten the cap on the bottle of bubbles?

How was I supposed to know that it wasn't a good idea to turn on the faucets full force to wash the bubble stuff down the drain?

So what if they were "good" towels? Was I supposed to let bubbles keep pouring onto the floor while I searched for "bad" ones?

If those towels are so special, how come Eva and Isabel use them?

Why do these things always happen to me? (Is it the red hair? Or the weird gene that skipped the rest of my family and picked me?)

Scratch out Plans A and B. On to Plan C: for Creative? or for Convincing? Hope I do *not have to go through the entire alphabet before my parents let me bike to the festival. I will be eighty by the time I get to Z.*

Plan C will not involve water or soap.

Abby tiptoed downstairs. Her family was still sleeping. For once, she was the first one up. Her bed was made, her room was neat, and she was now about to make breakfast for the entire family.

This was one for the *Hayes Book of World Records,* she thought. "Earliest Rising on a Sunday Morning by Fifth-Grader."

The phone rang. Abby grabbed it.

"Hi, Jessica," she whispered.

"Are you up?" her friend asked.

"Sure. I've been up for an hour." Abby sniffed the air. It still smelled like bubble bath. Soon the smell of delicious pancakes would make her family forget all about last night's disaster. This time, her plan wasn't going to fail. Jessica, who was a good cook, was going to help her.

"Shall I come over?" Jessica asked.

"Sure," Abby whispered. "Remember: Plan C for Cooking."

"I'll be there in five minutes."

Abby went to the kitchen. She got out the pancake mix and the eggs. She found the measuring cup and measuring spoons. She took out the butter and maple syrup.

The back door opened. Jessica came in. She was bundled up in a coat and scarf. Her cheeks were red. "It's really cold outside." She wheezed as she spoke. "I wonder if it's going to snow. I bet they won't cancel the soccer game this afternoon."

She pulled out her asthma inhaler, aimed it at her mouth, and breathed in deeply. Then she glanced around the room. "Pancake mix? No way!"

"It's fast," Abby said. "It's good, too. Isabel makes pancakes from it all the time."

"I hate that stuff." Jessica cooked a meal for her mother and herself once a week. "I make pancakes from scratch."

Scratch? It sounded like chickens rooting around in the dirt. It sounded like one of Abby's messy math papers, where she had to cross everything out. It sounded like an itch or a bug bite.

It didn't sound like golden brown pancakes with butter and maple syrup.

"Are you sure?" Abby spoke carefully. She didn't

want to hurt Jessica's feelings. After all, she had come over at 7:30 A.M. on a Sunday morning to help Abby out. How many friends would do that? "I really need to impress my family. Especially after last night."

"This will do it," Jessica assured her. "Believe me, if they're used to pancakes from a mix, they'll go crazy over these."

"Crazy," Abby repeated doubtfully. "They already think I'm crazy."

"Don't worry. This will do the trick," Jessica promised. "Get out the baking powder, milk, flour, and sugar. If you have any fruit, we can throw that in, too."

Abby rummaged through the cupboards, pulling out boxes and cans and jars. Jessica found some mixing bowls and began to measure out flour and sugar.

Half an hour later, as the first pancakes were beginning to cook, Alex wandered into the kitchen. As usual in the morning, his hair stood straight up on his head. His pajama tops and bottoms did not match. He wore an old pair of slippers and carried a battered computer keyboard under his arm.

"What are you doing with that keyboard, Alex?"

Jessica asked. She was sitting at the table, leafing through a cookbook, while Abby flipped pancakes.

"Taking it apart," he said. "I want to see what's inside."

"Do you want pancakes?" Abby asked. "They're Jessica's special recipe."

"Okay." He yawned and shuffled over to the table.

"Are you still mad at Abby?" Jessica asked.

Alex made a face. "Naw."

Every day Alex seemed a little more friendly and a little less hurt. The thaw was slow but sure.

"Do you want blueberries in your pancakes?" Abby asked.

"Okay." He yawned again.

Abby sprinkled frozen berries into the batter, then spooned it onto the hot pan. She watched as the batter began to bubble, then flipped the pancakes to the other side the way Jessica had instructed her.

"Here, Alex," she said, handing him a plate. "Don't pour out half the bottle of maple syrup."

Alex grunted and reached for the comics.

The Hayes family members began to drift into the kitchen.

"What smells so good?" Abby's mother asked sleepily.

Sunday was the only day of the week on which Olivia Hayes slept past 6:30 A.M. In honor of the occasion, she wore her old blue terry bathrobe and a pair of fuzzy slippers that Abby had made her in fourth grade. "Do I smell coffee, too?"

"Yes!" Abby said. "Welcome to the Hayes-y Days Café!"

Eva came in, pulling a sweatshirt over her swimsuit. "Pancakes!" she exclaimed. "That's great. I have a meet in an hour and a half. This is just what I need."

Abby beamed. Her plan was working. Everyone in her family was thrilled. The pancakes were turning out perfectly. She hoped she and Jessica had made enough for everyone — including themselves. She couldn't wait to try a few!

"By the way, Abby," Eva continued, "that tub was sparkling. How did you do it? You really amaze me. She cleaned the bathroom last night, Mom."

"Yes, I know." Abby's mother looked up from the newspaper.

"I think she should do it more often." Eva smiled at Abby. "It smells really good in there, too."

Abby flushed. This was the last thing she needed — Eva reminding everyone of last night's disaster.

Jessica came to the rescue. "Does anyone want hot chocolate?" she said loudly. "I'll heat up some milk!"

"Me!" Alex yelled.

"Me, too," said her father, coming into the kitchen. He had on sweatpants and a sweatshirt. While Abby's mother said that Sunday was her lazy day to sleep late and read the paper, her father liked to jog first thing in the morning. "I'll take some with my coffee. Who made this wonderful breakfast?"

"We're eating at the Hayes-y Days Café," Abby's mother said with a smile. "Jessica and Abby are the chefs."

"It was Abby's idea," Jessica said.

"I couldn't have done it without Jessica," Abby said.

"Done what?" Isabel made a grand entrance, as she often did. She wore a long yellow skirt and a V-neck T-shirt. A silver necklace with blue glass flowers was around her neck. She had painted her fingernails yellow to match her skirt.

All Isabel needed, Abby thought, was a crown on her head and a scepter in her hand.

"They got up early and made breakfast," Abby's father said. "That's impressive, isn't it?"

Impressive. That was the word Abby had been

waiting to hear. "It's mature, too, Dad," she reminded him. "And responsible."

"What happened to the bubble bath?" Isabel interrupted, spearing a pancake with her fork. "I wanted to take a long, hot bath this morning but had to take a shower instead."

"Bubble bath?" Abby repeated.

She should have known that just when everything was going well, one of her SuperSibs would spoil it.

Last night, Isabel made a pain of herself by hovering over Abby and pointing out all the places she had forgotten to clean. Then she left for a play with her friends, missing the Great Bathtub Disaster.

Yet Isabel still brought it up! Did she have some kind of sisterly radar that allowed her to home in on the most painful subjects?

"Um, the bottle tipped over when I was cleaning the bathroom," Abby mumbled.

Jessica shot her a sympathetic look.

"The whole thing?" Isabel demanded.

Abby nodded. She wished she had been able to save just a capful of the horrid stuff. Then Isabel would have been soaking in the tub at this very minute, instead of embarrassing her in front of the entire Hayes family.

"Why were you cleaning the bathroom, anyway, Abby? I meant to ask you last night. It's Eva's turn, isn't it?"

"She was doing it as a favor to me," Eva said. "I'm watching Alex during the festival, you know."

"You made her clean the bathroom for you because of that?" Isabel demanded.

Eva's eyes narrowed, and her chin thrust forward stubbornly. "Yeah, I did. So what?"

"Don't take advantage," Isabel pronounced. "You should be ashamed of yourself. What's the big deal about taking Alex to the festival, anyway? I'm doing it."

Alex, who had been immersed in the comics, suddenly let out a piercing wail. "I don't want Eva and Isabel to take me to the festival! I want Abby!"

Eva and Isabel ignored him.

"Ashamed of myself? For what?" Eva spat. "She practically begged me to clean the bathroom! Right, Abby?"

"Wrong," Abby answered, but fortunately no one was listening. When the two SuperPowers of the Hayes family engaged in battle, the best tactic was to remain silent and invisible.

"Abby! Abby! I want Abby!"

The twin SuperSibs faced off, screaming insults to the background music of Alex's wail.

Their father shook his head and disappeared out the door. Their mother picked up her newspaper and coffee and went to sit in the living room, muttering about her one day of peace.

Abby turned off the stove and slowly backed out of the kitchen. Jessica followed her.

"I wish I was an only child!" Abby said.

Jessica nodded her head in sympathy.

The breakfast had been perfectly made. The pancakes were heavenly. The coffee and hot chocolate were excellent. But the fighting twins had spoiled it all. Now Alex was upset again, and her parents had been reminded several times of last night's disaster. All of Abby's hard work had been undone.

Chapter 7

Tuesday

"Anger is a short madness."
—Horace

Hat Calendar

Sometimes it's a long one. Alex wouldn't speak to me until breakfast on Monday. The twins were fighting when I left and fighting when I came home. Did they fight all day? Eva had a swimming match, so they had to stop for a few hours.

After cleaning up the kitchen, Jessica and I went over to her house (certified sibling free). We played soccer in the afternoon, and our team won. I almost made a

Certified Sibling Free

point! It was freezing on the field! But better than being at my house.

I wanted to stay at Jessica's for a week, but I had to go home and think up Plan D.

Plan C was Catastrophic, Cataclysmic, and Calamitous. All these words point to Disaster. That is <u>not</u> what I want for Plan D.

Plan D must be Daring, Decisive, and Dynamic.

Hayes Book of World Records

A. Hayes has continued her quest for the world record in Uninterrupted Bed Making (sixteen days), as well as Neat Room Kept by a Messy Person (more than two weeks), and the special Good Loser Award When Playing Chess with Boy Genius (twenty-five games). In addition, she is trying for the record for Most Promising Plan That Completely Flopped (Sunday's breakfast).

(Shall I add a category for Longest Time to Decide on a Costume for Fifth-Grade Birthday Party? I might win that one, too!)

Costume idea #2: Be invisible.

This is what Natalie should be. Then she could go to Brianna's birthday party with Jessica and me. I asked my mother to talk to her mother, but she said that every family had its own rules, and we couldn't tell other families what to do.

Natalie's family's rules are unfair! I told Natalie about my Declaration of Independence, but she shook her head and said it wouldn't work in her family. It would just make things worse.

She is embarrassed because she is the only person in the fifth grade who can't go — just because it's a boy-girl party. She asked Jessica and me not to tell ANY-ONE!

We told her we would guard her secret with our lives. (Question: How do lives guard a secret? I don't understand.)

At least Natalie can meet us at the festival.

Speaking of the festival, my father said

this morning, "You're trying hard, Abby, and your mother and I appreciate it."

"Does that mean I have permission to bike to the festival?"

"Not yet," he said, "but keep up the good work."

First sign that Plans A, B, and C have not been complete failures. Must put renewed effort into Plan D.

I said to my father, "Everyone in my class is going on their own. Jessica, Brianna, Bethany, Zach, Tyler, Rachel, Meghan, and Jon are all going to the festival by themselves and with their friends. They don't have to prove how mature they are, either. Their parents just know!"

(I didn't mention Natalie.)

My father answered, "You still have to show us that you're responsible enough to be trusted on your own."

Natalie, Jessica, and I took a vote and decided that Jessica has the best family situation. She has no siblings and only one parent, who is not too strict.

Natalie told us that she has an older brother. We were surprised because she has never mentioned him before. He doesn't live with her family except on vacations and in the summer. He goes to boarding school. His name is Nicholas. She said he is even more annoying than the twin SuperSibs. That is hard to imagine.

"Everybody get out paper and pencil for the math quiz," Ms. Kantor announced.

Abby groaned. She hated math, and especially math quizzes. They were just too hard! Alex, on the other hand, could do math problems in his sleep, and probably did. Isabel got great marks in everything. When the fairy godmother handed out math genes in the Hayes family, she had skipped Abby's cradle. Abby couldn't figure out how she had missed her! Her red hair was like a flashing light.

She raised her hand. "Ms. Kantor? How come we have so many math quizzes?"

Ms. Kantor cleared her throat. "To prepare you for the statewide math tests at the end of the year."

"In third grade, I placed in the ninety-eighth percentile," Brianna said. She glanced at Zach. "That's nationwide."

"Yay, Brianna," Bethany said.

If there was a national bragging standard, Brianna would be in the one-hundredth percentile.

"I hate those state tests," Abby muttered.

"All right, no more discussion," Ms. Kantor said. "I want all of you to score in the ninety-ninth percentile by the end of the year. That includes you, Abby. I know you can do it." She passed out the quizzes.

Abby stared at the sheet full of fractions and ratios.

Fortunately, she had studied the night before.

Unfortunately, she had already forgotten everything she studied.

When it came to math, her brain was like a colander. Math facts ran through it like water.

Natalie and Jessica were bent over their work. So were Brianna and Bethany, Zach and Tyler, and most of the rest of the class.

"Concentrate! Concentrate!" Abby told herself sternly. She couldn't bring home a failing mark in math. Her parents wouldn't consider it a sign of maturity and responsibility.

She began to multiply and divide. When Ms. Kantor collected the tests, she had finished all the problems but one.

"That's the way, Abby!" Ms. Kantor said. "Good work!"

Abby tried to smile. Just because she had finished the quiz didn't mean she had gotten the right answers.

Ms. Kantor walked to the blackboard. Her long skirt swished around her ankles. She was wearing sneakers and ankle socks. They weren't fashionable like Ms. Bunder's combat boots, but Ms. Kantor said they were comfortable. "Okay, let's go over our spelling words now," she announced. "Any volunteers to give me a sentence with 'fragile'? Jessica?"

Jessica stood up. "The environment is very fragile."

"Good," Ms. Kantor said. "The next word is 'absolutely.' Bethany?"

"Brianna's birthday party will be absolutely the best," Bethany said.

Bethany's answer was absolutely obvious, Abby thought. She glanced over at Natalie who was scribbling on her social studies notebook. She wished that the B/Bs would stop talking about the party. Every time they did, Natalie looked upset.

"Abby?" Ms. Kantor said. "Can you give me a sentence with the word 'resistance'?"

"Um, yes." Abby stared at the blackboard. This is what happened when she didn't pay attention in class. She hoped that Ms. Kantor wouldn't send a note home about it.

"Resistance," she said slowly. "Parents have too much resistance to giving their kids freedom."

"Very good!" Ms. Kantor beamed at her.

Abby breathed a sigh of relief. Sometimes things worked out even when she wasn't trying hard.

If only it would happen that way with her family! One morning she would come down to breakfast, and her parents would announce that they were giving her permission to go to the festival with her friends. No more beds to make or tubs to scrub or chess games to be suffered with Alex. Nothing further to prove.

Why couldn't everything be as easy as making up sentences?

Chapter 8

Thursday

"What you can do, or think
you can do, begin it."

—Goethe

Egret Calendar

Do I have to finish it, too?

Things I have begun in the last few
days:

taking out garbage,
sorting bottles,
cans, and
cardboard
for recycling,
organizing summer clothes to
put upstairs in attic,
vacuuming living room floor

Things I have finished:
my homework

Costume idea #3: The "I Forgot to Get a Costume" Costume. Go as yourself. Act like this is an original idea.

The Roving Reporter in the Schoolyard
News flash! Today at recess, Abby Hayes did a survey of her classmates on the back playground.

"What are your favorite techniques to get what you want from your parents?" our investigating journalist asked. "Please share them with your fellow fifth-graders for the good of humankind."

The following are the results of her survey.

Begging, whining, and pouting: 3 (extremely annoying to parents)
Yelling and throwing fits: 1 (This can backfire.)
Arguing: 12 (a clear majority)
Sulking in room: 3 (not always fun)

"Everyone else does/has it": 7 (Parents are on to this argument, but we all use it anyway.)

Nagging: 2 (Doing this until parents give in requires great strength of character.)

Did you know that Ms. Kantor's fifth-graders had such a range of talents? Every single fifth-grader has mastered all of these difficult methods. These so-called "kids" are able to switch techniques with lightning swiftness. They often work best in combination.

Brianna revealed her version of the one, two, three knockout. "First I ask. If that doesn't work, I pout. Then I throw a screaming fit. That always does it."

Brianna (B for Best) then demonstrated her pout. It was indeed world-class. If there was a Pouting Olympics, Brianna would take the gold medal.

When arguing with her mother, Jessica has taken the words "why?" and "because" to new heights.

When Zach wants something, he doesn't stop talking about it until he gets it.

Bethany demonstrated her tearful, wide-eyed look, which changes to sullen fury in an instant.

Only Natalie admitted that none of these methods work for her.

The investigative reporter is now investigating whether she can apply these methods to her own situation. Should she try to wear her parents down, throw a screaming fit, or sulk for hours to get permission to go to the festival on her own? No, perhaps not. Paul and Olivia Hayes would not consider this mature behavior.

Thursday was always Abby's favorite day of the week. If she had her way, she would color it purple. That was the day that Ms. Bunder came to teach creative writing to Ms. Kantor's fifth-graders.

Nothing could ever make Thursday into a bad day!

"Did everyone write haiku poems?" Ms. Bunder asked soon after she arrived in the classroom.

"Yes!" the class responded.

"Let's put them on the board," Ms. Bunder suggested. She was wearing wide-legged pants of a shiny gray material and a beaded shirt. Thin silver wires with blue-and-green glass beads hung around her neck. Sometimes Abby couldn't believe that she was a teacher and not a classmate of Isabel or Eva's.

"Did anyone write about nature?" Ms. Bunder asked.

Abby raised her hand. "I wrote about the Great Bathtub Disaster," she said. "A disaster is natural, isn't it? It involved lots of water."

"Okay, Abby, you may put your poems on the board."

When she was done, Brianna raised her hand. "Ms. Bunder! I wrote about playing soccer."

"I wrote a poem about Brianna," said Bethany. "Also about my hamster."

Ms. Bunder motioned them up to the board.

Rain and mud do not stop me
I am the captain
I am the best.

by Brianna

Next to her, Bethany wrote:

Squeak, squeak
Hamster runs around on his wheel
He keeps me up at night.

I am Brianna's best friend.
She is the coolest.
Yay, Brianna.

Jessica leaned toward Abby. "I like Bethany's poem about the hamster but not the one about Brianna," she whispered.

"Maybe she should switch the words 'hamster' and 'Brianna,' " Abby whispered back.

One by one, the other students went up and copied their poems on the board. Then they returned to their seats.

Ms. Bunder nodded as she read them. "This is a very creative class," she said. "Does anyone have any comments?"

Brianna raised her hand.

"Yes, Brianna?"

"I like Zach's poem." She giggled. "It's so . . . poetic!" In a dramatic voice, Brianna recited:

"The screen flickers.
Lights flash.
I am happy."

"Do you want to talk about your poem, Zach?"
Ms. Bunder asked.

Zach stood up. "It's about turning on the computer." He sat down again.

"I'd like to print that in my family newsletter," Brianna said.

Zach shook his head.

"Why not?" Brianna demanded.

"You can print mine, Brianna," Bethany said.

Brianna ignored her best friend. "I want Zach's!"

"No," Zach said. "Sorry."

Abby opened her journal.

If Brianna put Zach's poem in her family newsletter, would she say that he's her boyfriend? Probably. I don't think Zach would like that. No wonder he said no.

Is Brianna going to pout to make him give her his poem? No. Pouting is for parents, not for friends. She looks mad, though.

Doesn't Zach get bored thinking and talking and writing about computers all the time? And why does Brianna think he's so cute?

Natalie says it's Zach's blue eyes and blond hair. Jessica says it's because he's the only boy in the class who ignores Brianna. Now Bethany is starting to like Tyler. Is it because he is the best friend of her best friend's crush?

When Ms. Bunder said what a creative class we were, she looked right at me! She must have liked my poems about the Great Bathtub Disaster!

Abby's Wish List

I wish Ms. Bunder were my teacher for EVERY subject. (Even though I like Ms. Kantor, too.)

I wish I could write about making my bed or putting away my clothes instead of doing it.

I wish I could write to prove to my parents how mature I am!

I wish I could write a costume for Brianna's party.

Maybe I should go to Brianna's birthday party as a poem! Ha-ha (costume idea #4).

After everyone had finished reading the poems, Ms. Bunder collected them. "We'll write more," she promised. "At the end of the year we'll choose our best work and put it into a book. Maybe we can have a poetry reading for your families."

"Yes!" Abby said, pumping her fist.

It would be a chance for her family to see her shine. After all, this was her best subject, her favorite class, and her most-loved teacher. Too bad she had to wait until spring for it to happen!

Chapter 9

Thursday evening

"Do the work you love and
love the work you do."

This isn't from a calendar. It's one of
my mom's favorite sayings. I hear it all
the time!

My mom loves her work. She has wanted
to be a lawyer since she was nine. Dad
loves his work, too, even though he was
more than thirty when he started it.

(Were there personal computers around
when Dad was a kid? He says no. I
wonder if Zach and Tyler know how lucky
they are? If they had been born a few
years earlier, they would have missed computers. Then what would they have done?)

* * *

If adults love their work, why can't kid work be fun, too?

List of household chores I enjoy:

Okay. Never mind.

Hayes Household Update

At dinner tonight, Isabel Hayes lectured about checks and balances. (Note: Certain members of the Hayes family thought she was discussing a bank account. She was  actually talking about the federal government.) Eva Hayes, captain of swim team, basketball team, and lacrosse team, said her teams will sponsor an auction at the festival. Prizes will be donated by families and businesses. Olivia Hayes will donate an hour of free legal advice.

Abby Hayes would like to win it. She would like to sue her family for the right to go to the festival.

Paul and Olivia Hayes have not yet made up their minds. The festival is only two weeks away!!!

The Hayes family will be very busy this weekend. On Saturday, Olivia Hayes will run a marathon race to raise money for sick children.

Paul Hayes will be out of town all weekend on important business.

Isabel Hayes has a debate, and Eva Hayes has a swim meet.

That leaves Abby and Alex Hayes. They have no particular activities.

Olivia Hayes must find someone to watch them.

After dinner, Abby helped her mother stack the dishes in the dishwasher.

"Wow!" she said, almost dropping a plate as the idea roared through her.

As brainstorms went, it was not a one or two. It

wasn't a skimpy, puny, thunder-and-lightning brainstorm. It was a full-fledged, gale-force, number-ten hurricane that blew everything away. "Mom, I have a solution to all your problems!"

"What?" her mother said.

"Since I don't have a soccer game this weekend, I can baby-sit for Alex on Saturday."

"You, Abby?"

"Yes, me. I'm ten years old and in fifth grade," Abby announced, as if her mother didn't know. She did, but sometimes it was good to remind her. "If I take care of Alex, you won't have to find a baby-sitter."

Abby's mother gave her a searching look. "Do you think you can do it? You'll have to watch him, entertain him, and feed him for an entire afternoon. You can't quit if you get tired or bored or annoyed."

"I won't," Abby promised. "Aren't I used to playing with Alex? I can fix peanut butter and jelly sandwiches and take him to the park if the weather is good. If it isn't, we'll do projects at home."

"Will you watch him carefully?"

"Mom! I know the rules of safety. I won't answer the door or tell strangers that we're home alone. I'll make sure that Alex doesn't play with matches, or use the stove, or cross the street by himself."

Her father came into the kitchen with a cup of coffee.

"What do you think, Paul?" her mother asked. "Should we allow Abby to watch Alex this Saturday?"

Abby held her breath.

He took a sip of coffee. "All by herself?"

"I'll check in with the neighbors," Abby said. "And I can call Jessica's mom if I need help."

"It's not a bad idea," her father said. "How much do you charge?"

She thought for a moment. "A dollar fifty an hour. That's what Jessica gets when she baby-sits for the kids next door."

"What a bargain," her father said, winking at her.

Her mother nodded her head.

"And if I'm mature enough to watch Alex, you have to let me go to the festival with my friends," she added quickly.

Her parents exchanged glances.

"Sounds fair to me," her father said.

"Agreed," her mother said. "You have a deal."

HOORAY!! HOORAY!! *No more horrible household chores! No more Great Bathtub Disasters or Battling Breakfasts! No more worrying about how to prove I'm trustworthy and mature! I can baby-sit, and get permission to go to the festival, AND get paid, too!*

Plan E stands for Excellent, Exceptional, and Exactly What Is Needed.

Things I Promised to Do with Alex When Baby-Sitting

Rollerblading, biking, picnicking in the park (if it's not too cold), computer games, chess, reading his favorite books out loud for as long as he likes, and letting him take down all my calendars to play with.

"So?" he said.

Alex Hayes is not cooperating.
It is not fair.

❋   ❋   ❋

"We can make brownies together," I finally promised, "and we'll put ice cream sundaes on top of them. With cherries, nuts, and chocolate candies."

"Okay," Alex said. "You win."

"I just want us to have fun together," I said.

Is this what it's like to be a parent? Arguing is exhausting. No wonder mothers and fathers are so tired all the time!

Alex and I will have fun together. My parents will be grateful. I will earn money and go to the festival with my friends.

(Repeat one hundred times at dawn, dusk, and midnight.)

Chapter 10

Oh, yeah? You can't be true to yourself if you're a ten-year-old. You have to do what everyone tells you to do! Or else you're in big trouble.

Costume ideas #5, #6, #7, #8: Go as a zero. Go as a world record. Go as a gold record. Or a record company. Go as a lightbulb (for ideas). Go as. . . . Oh, go get a snack!

New Category for the <u>Hayes Book of World Records</u>: Most Costume Ideas for Brianna's Birthday Party.

Also, Most Throwaway Costume Ideas for Brianna's Birthday Party.

<u>What I Am Doing to Get Ready for Baby-sitting Alex This Weekend</u>

Hid brownie mix so no one will use it before tomorrow.

Pushed ice cream to back of freezer so Tsabel won't eat it tonight.

Found cherries, whipped cream, and nuts. Hid them.

Gathered Rollerblades, knee and wrist pads, and helmets into one pile.

Unlocked bikes.

Started using throat lozenges. Vocal cords must be in fine shape for non-stop reading.

Deep knee bends and push-ups.

Say "Alex, honey" every chance I get. Ruffle his hair. Smile at him a lot.

It was the end of the school day. Ms. Kantor's fifth-grade class put on their jackets, shouldered their backpacks, and got in line at the door.

"Hey, quit pushing me," Tyler said to Zach.

"I didn't do it," Zach protested.

Bethany giggled. She was wearing a white fleece pullover and a short embroidered skirt. "It was me. I bumped into you by accident. Sorry."

"Oh," Tyler said. He fiddled with a strap on his backpack. "Hey. I've been meaning to ask you. What's your hamster's name?"

"Blondie," Bethany said. "Do you like hamsters?"

"Sure," Tyler replied. "They're furry."

Bethany giggled again. "What are you doing after school?"

"You promised to come over to my house, Bethany," Brianna interrupted. She had on a pale blue peacoat over a dark red skirt. "We have to go over the party plans. The entire fifth grade is coming."

At the back of the line, Abby nudged Natalie. "Does Brianna know yet?" she whispered.

"No," Natalie whispered back. "I keep hoping my parents will change their minds."

"What if they don't?" Jessica asked.

"I'll pretend I'm sick," Natalie said.

Abby zipped up her jacket. She wished Natalie could go to the party. It just wasn't fair!

"Make up a good disease," she advised Natalie. "Maybe you can come down with Purple Lightning Madness that causes you to read Harry Potter books over and over again."

Natalie ran her hands through her short black hair and smiled. "That's what I'll be doing on the day of the party, reading Harry Potter books."

"Did someone say Harry Potter?" Zach asked. "I just started the first book. It's great!"

"It was me," Natalie said.

"Have you read them all?" he asked her.

"Fourteen times each," she replied.

"That's awesome," he said.

The bell rang. School was over for the week. The fifth-graders began to rush into the hallway.

"One at a time! Quietly!" Ms. Kantor called. She stood at the door and said good-bye to each student as they left.

"Have a great weekend," she said to Abby.

"I'm baby-sitting my little brother all Saturday afternoon."

"That's a lot of responsibility," Ms. Kantor said.

"I can handle it," Abby said.

As the fifth-graders spilled out onto the play-ground, Brianna gathered a circle of her classmates around her.

"Has everyone figured out their costumes?" she demanded. "The party's only nine days away."

"Nope," Abby said, yanking her bucket hat over her ears. It had gotten colder while they were in school. She hated when the days got colder instead of warmer.

Brianna turned to Zach and Tyler. "What about you two?"

"I'm not telling," Zach said.

"Me, neither," Tyler echoed.

"Natalie?" Brianna asked. "I hope you're planning something good. You've never been to one of my parties before. It'll be a real treat for you."

Natalie shuffled her feet. "I'm planning something very special," she mumbled.

"Like what?" Bethany said. "Tell us."

"It's a . . . it's a . . ." Natalie glanced desperately around the playground. "It . . . it . . ."

"It's a three-part costume," Jessica jumped in. "She's going with me and Abby. We're going to be . . ."

"Three links of a chain," Abby finished.

Brianna looked confused. "Three links of a chain? What kind of a costume is that?"

"Just a joke," Abby said. "We're really going to be a fork, knife, and spoon." It was the first thing out of her mouth. She hadn't thought about it at all.

"That's funny," Bethany said.

"It's easy to make, too," Abby said. Come to think of it, it was a pretty good idea. "You just need lots of aluminum foil and duct tape. And some cardboard."

"I'm going to spend all weekend working on my costume," Brianna said. "I bet everyone else will, too."

Natalie tried to smile.

"Me, too!" Bethany chirped. "Yay for Brianna's party!"

On the way home, Natalie thanked Abby and Jessica for keeping her secret. "But what will Brianna say when I don't show up?" she worried. "She expects a knife, fork, and spoon. What if only a knife and a spoon arrive at the party?"

"I'll tell her we forgot to wash you," Abby said. "You got left in the sink."

Natalie laughed.

"Anyway, we might not even be silverware for Brianna's party. We might surprise everyone with another idea."

"I want to be a spoon," Jessica said. "I'm sick of always being an astronaut or an alien. It's so obvious."

"Okay, I'll be the knife," Abby agreed. It solved her costume problem — finally!

"I wish you could come," Jessica said to Natalie.

"Besides, we need you," Abby added. "Without a fork, a knife and spoon can't eat anything besides pudding."

Natalie kicked at the fallen leaves covering the sidewalk. "I'll tell my parents that," she joked. "That'll convince them."

They reached Jessica's house. "Want to stay for a few minutes?" she asked.

They sat down on the porch steps. Jessica offered everyone a piece of a chocolate bar. They munched on chocolate and watched other kids walking home. Abby pulled out her journal.

If Brianna learns that Natalie's parents won't let her go, she will probably brag that she has the best parents in the fifth grade. Brianna can turn anything into a brag. How many years of hard work and sacrifice did it take her to develop this talent?

Will create special category in the <u>Hayes Book of World Records for Natalie</u>: Most Harry Potter Books Read by Fifth-Grader.

Will this be consolation for not going to party?

I don't think so.

Chapter 11

Saturday morning

"Even if you're on the right track, you'll get run over if you just sit there."

—Will Rogers

Lawn Ornaments Calendar

No chance of me getting run over! My baby-sitting day will not have much sitting in it.

Plan E is the Plan to End All Plans. Alex and I will have an Exciting, Energetic, Eventful Day, which will persuade my parents what an Extremely Mature and Responsible Ten-Year-Old I am!

Everything will go well. My parents will be elated. I will be exhausted, but who cares, because next week is the festival!!!

Abby's mother pinned her keys to the waistband of her shorts. She pulled on a sweatshirt, picked up her water bottle, and said, for the hundredth time, "Now you know what to do, don't you, Abby?"

"Yes, Mom," Abby repeated. "If there's an emergency or if I have a question, I'll call the neighbors or Jessica's mom. I won't let anyone know that you and dad are gone, and I won't answer the door."

"Right," her mother said. "Take good care of Alex, lock up if you go out, and don't use the stove."

"Yes, Mom." Abby had baked the brownies this morning. Now all she had to do was add ice cream, whipped cream, and cherries. She would make the sundaes at the end of the afternoon. That way, she'd have a treat to promise Alex if he was good. Jessica had given her that baby-sitting tip.

"Now, Alex," her mother said, "you have to cooperate with Abby. Remember, she's in charge."

"Uh-huh."

"We'll have a great time, Alex!" Abby put her arm around him. "I've got a whole afternoon of exciting activities planned."

Her mother smiled. "Put on your jackets if you go to the park. Abby, you can make peanut butter and jelly sandwiches for lunch, can't you?"

"Mom, I'm an expert on peanut butter and jelly," Abby protested.

Their mother gave them each a quick hug. "Be good," she said.

"Win the race!" Abby said.

"Raise lots of money for those kids," Alex added.

Their mother checked her watch. "Got to run!" she said with a laugh. "I really do this time."

Abby locked the door behind her mother and turned to face her younger brother. "It's just the two of us now, Alex. What do you want to do first? Chess? Bike riding? Rollerblading? The park?"

"I want lunch." Alex watched Abby as if he wasn't sure of what she was going to do next. At least he wasn't whining that he wanted Eva or Isabel to baby-sit. "Then I want to go to the park. Then I want to play chess, then computer games."

"Anything," Abby promised him. Her heart was beating fast. She had played with Alex a million times, but this was different. This was the first time she was in charge and responsible.

Forty-five minutes later, she was pushing Alex on the swings in the park.

Alex had been quiet at first, but now he was having a good time. "Push me harder!" he yelled. "Higher!"

Abby pushed with all her strength. He soared out, then swung back. "I'm flying!" he called.

She pushed him again and again and again. Her arms were tired, but she wasn't complaining. So far everything was going well. She and Alex had eaten peanut butter and jelly sandwiches together, then cleaned up the kitchen. Afterward, they had walked to the park.

Until she decided to go to the festival with her friends, Alex always said that Abby was his favorite sister. She knew he felt hurt about her desertion.

Today she would make it all up to him. They would have an unforgettable day together.

"That was good," he said, when he got off. "What do we do next?"

"The jungle gym?"

"I love the jungle gym!" Alex grabbed her hand and began to run toward it. "Bet you can't hang upside down."

"Oh, yeah?" Abby said.

He shimmied up to the top and hung there like a koala bear. "Can you do this?" he demanded.

Abby hung from her knees. "Can you do this?"

"Yes!" Alex cried. He flipped upside down, then pulled himself up and sat on top of the bars. Abby followed him.

"I'm having fun," Alex said.

Abby smiled. Just wait until her parents heard about what a good time they had! Wait until they saw the clean kitchen! She had even wiped the counters. Wait until they saw what good care she had taken of Alex! The festival was a sure thing. Nothing could keep her from it now.

She jumped off the jungle gym. "Let's go down the slide," she yelled. "Race you over there. On your mark, get set, GO!"

Running across the grass, Abby let out a whoop. She was in good shape from the weeks of soccer practice and all the training she had done. "I'm going to beat you!" she cried. "I'm faster, stronger, and better!"

"No, you're not!" Alex yelled. "I am!"

He was gaining on her. For a second-grader who spent most of his time in front of the computer, he sure was fast. Then again, even at her best she wasn't that fast for a fifth-grader. Playing soccer had improved her speed, but not much.

Maybe Alex had inherited Isabel's mind and Eva's sports genes. Thank goodness he was younger. An older SuperSib genius sports star was the last thing Abby needed.

"Can't stop me!" Alex sprinted past her, waving his arms.

"Nyah, nyah, I'll catch up!"

Alex ran even faster, turning to see whether Abby was gaining on him.

"I'm going to get you!" Abby yelled, putting on a burst of speed.

"No! Never!" Alex cried. With a wild whoop, he leaped forward and crashed straight into the slide.

At first Abby thought it was just a bump. Alex had gotten hundreds of them.

Then he turned toward her, cupping his face in his hands. Blood poured out between his fingers.

Abby's heart pounded. There was blood everywhere. She raced toward him. "Are you okay?" she cried. "Are you okay, Alex?"

He clutched his forehead. "No!" he shrieked. "No!"

She pulled off her scarf and pressed it against his head. In a moment, the scarf was soaked.

"I want Mom!" he cried.

"Okay, we'll get her. You're going to be all right," Abby said. It had to be true. She hoped it was true. "We'll get Mom," she repeated. She didn't know where. Right now her mother was thirty miles out of town and running a marathon around a lake.

Frantically, she looked for an adult. There was no one in sight, only a few kids on the swings.

She felt dizzy with fear. Where was the phone? Should she call an ambulance? She tried to remember what she had learned in summer camp about injuries. If it was an artery — but there weren't any arteries in the forehead. Could he faint from loss of blood? Could he die? There was so much blood!

Jessica . . . Her house was only a block away. Her mother was home. She would help them.

"Can you walk?" she asked Alex. Her voice was shaking.

In answer, he howled even more loudly. "Mom! Mom!"

She grabbed his arm and pulled him toward the street. She couldn't leave him here alone. She had to get him help.

"We're going to get Jessica's mom," she said loudly. "She'll know what to do."

A few minutes later, the two of them stumbled onto Jessica's porch. Blood trailed behind them on the sidewalk and stairs. Abby pressed the doorbell as hard as she could.

"What — " Jessica's mother began as she opened the door.

Abby pointed to her brother and burst into tears.

Jessica's mother took one look at Alex and grabbed her car keys from the stand by the door. "Jessica!" she yelled.

"Get in the car," she ordered Alex and Abby. "We're going to the emergency room."

In the car, Abby held Alex's hand. If he was okay, she thought, she would never get mad at him again, even if he won seventy games of chess in a row. She would go to the festival with him and do everything he wanted to do. She would never complain again about him wanting to do everything with her and Jessica.

She had let him down in the park. She shouldn't have raced him. She shouldn't have tried to beat him. If he was okay, she would let him win everything for the rest of his life.

"I'm sorry, Alex," she whispered. "I'm really sorry."

Chapter 12

Saturday evening

"Experience is the name everyone gives to their mistakes."

—Mark Twain

Wooden Raft Calendar

Boy, do I have a lot of experience! Too much, if you ask me.

Number of stitches Alex had to have in the emergency room: 14

Number of times I said, "It's all my fault!" 500 per minute

Number of times Jessica's mom tried to reassure me it wasn't: about the same

Number of times I believed her: 0

Number of ice-cream scoops eaten by Alex Hayes after his stitches: 3 large ones

Number of ice-cream scoops eaten by Abby Hayes: 0

(Note: This is the first time in recorded history that I have ever refused ice cream. But my stomach was so wobbly that I thought I was going to throw up.)

E is for Emergency. Why didn't I know that? F is for Failure and Forget about the Festival.

Missing the festival is the least of my problems! My parents will never trust me again! I will be lucky if they let me walk to school on my own! Or ride my bike around the block!

Maybe I am a Menace to Humanity. In the interests of public safety, I should stay in my room for the rest of my life.

At least Alex is going to be okay. (HOORAY!!!!) He has luckily survived what will probably be the only baby-sitting job I ever have.

When we got home, I made him change his clothes and put the dirty ones in the wash. My scarf is ruined, but who cares?

* * *

My mother is not home yet. Jessica and her mom are in the living room, playing board games with Alex. They are staying with us until my mother gets here.

I said, "I know. You don't trust me with Alex. I don't blame you."

Jessica's mom said, "Not at all, Abby! You're too upset to be left alone. I wouldn't want to be alone after taking my little brother to the emergency room."

New category for the <u>Hayes</u> <u>Book</u> of <u>World Records</u>: Nicest Person to Have Around in an Emergency. Jessica's mom.

What is my mother going to do when she walks in?

What I think will happen:

1. My mother will faint.

2. My mother will yell, cry, and shriek.

3. My mother will take away all my privileges for the rest of my life. She and my father will put me on a diet of bread and water. I will live alone in my prison

cell of a room, with only calendars to console me and mark the time.

What will probably happen:
1. My mother will be very disappointed in me.
2. My mother will be extremely angry at me.
3. I will be grounded for two weeks.
4. I will miss the festival and Brianna's birthday party.

Do you think I care about missing the festival or Brianna's party? NO! All those worries have been sucked out of me, as if a vacuum cleaner came and scooped out my insides.

I hear a car. It might be my mother.
It is my mother. . . .

I wish I had wings and could fly away.
I wish I had a cloak of invisibility and could disappear.

I wish I had the power to change shapes and could become a dog or a hamster for a few hours until my mother calms down.

I wish I were part of a fairy tale, so this would end happily ever after.

Abby's mother came into the house. Alex, Jessica, and her mom were in the living room.

"Where's Abby?" her mother cried. "Is she okay? I had a feeling something was wrong!"

Jessica's mom pointed to Alex's forehead. "He had an accident," she said. "We took him to the emergency room. He needed a few stitches, but he's fine now."

"Abby!" her mother called.

Abby came in slowly from behind the door.

Her mother had pulled Alex onto her lap. Jessica's mom and Jessica were on the floor in front of a board game. They weren't really playing, though.

"There you are, Abby," her mother said. She didn't sound too angry. "I'm glad to see you. Tell me what happened."

Abby gave her all the details. Then she waited for the worst.

I'm still so astonished, I can hardly write it down. My mother thanked me for having a cool head in an emergency.

(The cool head felt like a bunch of eggs getting scrambled.)

She said I had done exactly the right thing.

"But it was my fault!" I burst out. "If I hadn't been racing Alex, he wouldn't have hit his head on the slide!"

"How often have you raced Alex?" my mother asked quietly.

My face was hot. I didn't answer.

"Millions of times, I bet," my mother said.

"Yeah, I guess so."

"And how many times has he run into a slide?"

"Just once," I admitted.

"So you couldn't have known he would hit his head if you raced him," my mother concluded with a flourish.

I see why my mother is a successful lawyer. Unstoppable logic and good interrogation techniques.

She said she was glad everyone was okay. She said going to Jessica's house was exactly the right thing to do and that I had shown good sense. She said most kids got stitches at one time or another in their lives, and she hoped Alex had gotten them over with.

(Are stitches like chicken pox? I don't think so.)

"The doctor said I was the bravest seven-year-old she had ever seen!" Alex bragged.

Was glad to hear seven-year-old brother bragging. Not obnoxious as it is with Brianna. A sign of health and happiness.

"I used to jump off tables when I was four," my mother told us. "I broke my arm once and my leg twice. I had to get stitches when I crashed through the back door."

My mom invited Jessica and her mom to stay for dinner. We made spaghetti and salad and had brownies with ice cream (again!) for dessert. This time I ate everything.

Is this a fairy tale? The ending is "happily ever after." At least I think so. So much has happened today that I am exhausted. I want to sleep for a long time.

P.S. Alex and I did have an unforgettable afternoon together!

Chapter 13

Saturday morning

"Experience is the best teacher."

Pinwheel Calendar

I prefer Ms. Bunder to be my teacher! Or Ms. Kantor, or one of my parents, or even one of my SuperSisters!

Things I learned from Alex's accident:
The sight of blood makes me feel sick.
Don't race in parks without an adult around.
Always remind Alex to watch where he's going.
Parents are unpredictable. They get angry when you forget to take colored markers out

of your jeans pockets before putting them in the wash and other dumb things like that.

When it comes to something really important, though, like accidents and blood and stitches, they're understanding and calm. (Does this happen all the time with everyone's parents? Or was I just lucky? I don't want to test this idea out!)

TODAY IS THE FESTIVAL! I CAN BIKE THERE WITH JESSICA! I HAVE EIGHT DOLLARS TO SPEND! HOORAY!

This is a very exciting weekend. First the festival and then, tomorrow morning, Jessica and I are going to do our costumes for Brianna's party. Natalie is going to help us. Then she will go home where she will be suddenly stricken by Spotted Newt Fever or Mongoose Pox or Purple Lightning Madness, which will force her to cancel her appearance as a fork at Brianna's Best Birthday Bash.

"There will be a tall, dark stranger in your life," Isabel predicted to Abby in the hallway of the Hayes house. She was dressed as a fortune-teller in a silver vest, worn over a red embroidered blouse and a long velvet skirt. She had put on gold earrings, lots of makeup, and for the occasion had newly painted her fingernails to match her blouse.

"When?" Abby said.

The doorbell rang. Alex ran to open the door. "It's Jessica!" he cried. "She's on her bike! It's time to leave for the festival!"

"My prediction has come true," Isabel said in her most mysterious voice.

"Jessica's tall and dark, but not a stranger," Abby joked.

"Two out of three isn't bad," Isabel said. "I bet most fortune-tellers don't get it right that often."

Jessica wiped her feet on the mat. She was wearing boot-leg jeans and a heavy fleece sweater. Her gloves and socks were rainbow-striped. Her bike helmet dangled over her arm. "I like your costume, Isabel!"

Isabel took Jessica's hand. "For your kind words, I will read your fortune for free." She traced her finger over the knitted fabric of Jessica's glove. "I see red. . . . I see blue. . . . You will lead a very colorful life," she concluded.

"Gee," Jessica said. "What if I had worn my white mittens?"

Abby tied the laces of her sneakers into multiple knots so they wouldn't catch in the gearshift of her bike. She checked her pockets to make sure she had her money. Then she picked up her bike helmet and adjusted the straps.

"Have you got your stitches out yet?" Jessica asked Alex.

"Yep." He pointed to his forehead.

"That's some scar," Jessica said admiringly.

"Everyone in second grade is jealous." Abby fastened the strap of her helmet. "No one else at Lancaster Elementary has a mean-looking scar like that."

Alex struck a karate pose. "I got it in a laser fight with the forces of darkness!"

"The evil Slide Master got you," Abby said, grabbing him in a hug.

"Good-bye," her father said, giving her a kiss at the door. "I'm really proud of you, Abby."

"For what?"

"For inviting Alex to bike with you and Jessica to the festival. That shows a lot of maturity."

"Really?" I said.

"Yes," her father said. "You're growing up."

Abby's mother nodded her head.

"We'll be there in half an hour or so. Ride safely, especially when you cross the street."

"Of course, Mom!" Abby promised. "We'll be very careful."

"We know you will," her parents said.

Abby turned to her little brother. "Ready, Alex?"

"Yes!" Alex said. He tightened his helmet strap, then reached into his pocket and pulled out a five-dollar bill. "Look how much I got to spend!"

"That should be enough to stuff yourself with cotton candy," Abby observed.

The three of them got on their bikes.

"Don't worry, Mom and Dad, we won't let him ride into any slides!" They pedaled down the street toward the high school.

The first thing Abby, Jessica, and Alex saw when they entered the high school gymnasium was a six-year-old girl throwing wet sponges at the gym teacher, Mr. Stevens, who stood behind a screen with only his head showing.

He wasn't too wet, at least not yet. Zach and Tyler were standing in line with their tickets. "We're going to get him soaked," they promised.

"Okay, hit me with your best shot!" Mr. Stevens encouraged the girl.

"My dad did that last year," Abby said. "He got really drenched."

"Smart guy," Mr. Stevens commented, "not to do it again this year."

They passed a table of brownies, cakes, and muffins for sale, then another where kids were making candy-coated apples.

"There's Natalie!" Alex yelled.

She sat at the face-painting booth, having her face decorated with green leaves.

"Nice foliage," Abby said.

"Thanks!" Natalie peered into the mirror at the green leaves trailing over her face. "Isn't this fun?"

"I want flames on my face," Jessica announced.

"We can do that." It was Bethany's mother. She didn't look anything like Bethany, except the shape of her eyes. She was wearing jeans and a sweatshirt and sneakers, not the kind of clothes that Bethany wore.

Bethany's mom picked up a paintbrush, dabbed it

in orange-red paint, and began to draw flames going up Jessica's cheeks. "How about you? Do you want flames, too?" she asked Abby. "Or do you want leaves? I can do butterflies or cats or rainbows, too."

"I definitely don't want flames," Abby said. "My hair already looks like it's on fire!"

Alex tugged at Abby's hand. "I want to be a robot," he said.

"You're next," Bethany's mom promised him. "I have lots of silver makeup waiting just for you."

He sat down. She smoothed silver face paint expertly over his skin, then gave him large square eyes, a straight red mouth, and a green nose.

"Hey, Alex!" It was Eva. There was a bag of brightly colored balls slung over her shoulder. "Ready to come with me?"

"I — am — a — robot," Alex said in a mechanical voice. "I — am — dangerous."

He gave Abby a quick hug and then took Eva's hand. "Take — me — to — your — leader."

With a wave, they disappeared into the crowd.

It was Abby's turn to have her face painted. "Can you put smile faces all over my face?" she asked Bethany's mom. "That way, even if I don't feel like smiling, I'll still look friendly," she explained to her friends.

As Bethany's mom put the last smile on the last round yellow circle, Paul Hayes appeared with his video camera. "Let me get a shot of you, girls!" he said. "You look great!"

Natalie, Jessica, and Abby put their arms around each other and mugged for the camera.

"Terrific!" Abby's father said. He lowered the camera. "Did Eva take Alex?"

"They left a few minutes ago," Abby said.

Her father picked up his camera again as a group of kids in animal masks passed by. "Well, enjoy yourselves, girls! You're on your own now."

The three girls hugged each other again.

"We're on our own now!" Abby repeated. "Yes!"

Saturday night.

Number of predictions Isabel made at the festival: 357

Number that have come true: 0

Number of predictions that Isabel says will come true: all of them (If so, she will get a category in the

<u>Hayes Book of World Records</u>.)

Number of times Zach and Tyler hit Mr. Stevens with a sponge: 5

Number of sit-ups he has threatened to make them do next week in gym class: 700 (Ha-ha. I think he's joking.)

Amount of fun we had: A LOT!!!

Natalie even said the festival almost made up for not being able to go to Brianna's party tomorrow.

Chapter 14

Sunday

"Friendship is the finest flower in the garden of life."

Marigold Calendar

Is friendship a flower? If so, Jessica would start wheezing every time she saw me. She is allergic to most flowers!

Yesterday was the festival; today is Brianna's birthday party. This weekend is an embarrassment of riches, as Isabel likes to say.

I wonder why riches are an embarrassment. A happiness of riches or a joy of riches is more like it.

"Here we are," Abby's mother said as she pulled up to Brianna's house. It was big and white, with a landscaped yard. "Have a good time at the party."

Jessica and Abby got out of the car. Abby was wearing dark pants for the butter knife handle. She had made the blade from cardboard and taped it on with duct tape. Jessica was dressed all in gray. She had a round spoon top. Both girls had painted their faces silver. They were carrying brightly wrapped presents.

"I got Brianna a ballet dancer calendar," Abby said as they walked up to the door. "What did you get?"

"My mom and I bought her a mirror and hairbrush set."

"A mirror — that's the perfect gift for Brianna," Abby agreed.

They rang the bell. The door swung open.

"Welcome to Brianna's birthday party!" Brianna greeted them. She was dressed in a green satin gown with large pink brocade flowers and a long velvet sash. On her head she wore a tiara of fake diamonds.

"Ooooh, presents! I love presents!" she squealed.

"They're for you," Abby said. "Happy birthday."

Brianna took the presents. "I'm so sorry about Natalie," she said. "It's such a shame."

"Yes," Abby and Jessica chorused.

"I hope she didn't spread it to everyone yesterday at the festival," Bethany said. She was dressed as a mouse in white fur, with a hood and pink ears.

"No," they said together.

"Pinkeye is such a contagious disease," Brianna said. "I've never had it!"

"She got medicine," Abby said. "You know, those antibiotic eyedrops. They work really fast. She'll be better tomorrow."

In the next room, someone banged a drum. A clarinet squawked. Someone turned up an amplifier, then turned it down again.

"You got here just in time for the music. Come on!" Brianna waved Abby and Jessica into the living room.

Crepe paper spirals crisscrossed the room; shiny balloons hung everywhere; winking lights outlined the ceiling and windows. At one end of the room was a long table piled with food: pizza cut into tiny triangles, miniature hot dogs, bowls of popcorn, candy kisses, fruit punch, five different kinds of soda, and platters of grapes and strawberries.

Almost the entire class was there. Everyone was in

costume. There were fairies, dancers, pirates, ghosts, and a few cartoon characters. There was also a cat, a mailbox, a computer Web site, and a giant grape.

The band began to play.

"Want a kiss?" Brianna held up a silver-wrapped candy to Zach.

"Uh, no thanks." Zach had white hair and a suit jacket and was bent over a cane.

"You're sure? Not even for the birthday girl?"

He shook his head. A shower of white powder fell on his shoulders. "Look. Dandruff. I put flour in my hair to make it white."

"That's disgusting, Zach." Brianna unwrapped the kiss and popped it into her own mouth. "I hope you don't get flour all over the living room! It'll make my mom crazy."

Brianna's mom carried a bowl of potato chips to the food table. She was wearing a tight, short skirt and a bright blue jacket. Her hair was short and styled. Her lipstick was red; her high heels matched her jacket.

"She looks like a model, not a mom," Abby whispered to Jessica.

"Having fun at our little party?" Brianna's mom asked Tyler, who was wearing an ape suit.

He swung his arms and hiccuped. "Sure," he said.

"Let's dance!" Brianna cried.

No one moved.

Brianna put her hands on her hips. "Doesn't anyone want to dance?"

"You go first, Brianna," her mother encouraged her. "After all, you've been dancing since you were two years old."

Brianna waved her arms gracefully and then began to do a complicated dance step across the floor. "Come on, everyone! Zach, dance with me!"

"I'm too old," he croaked.

After a few minutes, Bethany hip-hopped out onto the floor in her white mouse costume to join her best friend. Tyler swung his arms wildly and leaped in front of her.

Pretty soon everyone was dancing. Even Zach threw away his cane and joined in.

"Isn't this the best party ever?" Brianna yelled.

"Yay, Brianna!" Bethany called. "You're the best!"

Sunday night.
Brianna's party was good! Dancing in costumes was a lot of fun. Some people couldn't move too well, like the grape and

the mailbox (Meghan and Rachel), while others, like Zach and Tyler, danced in character. Tyler made a lot of ape motions and noises, which was pretty obnoxious, while Zach pretended that his bones were aching, which was funny. Jessica and I made up a knife-and-spoon dance.

When we were done dancing, Brianna's mom brought out the birthday cake. It was a vanilla layer cake decorated with a picture of a ballerina and a soccer goal in the background and said, in pink icing: "Happy birthday, Brianna! Always strive to be the best!"

We all got miniature soccer balls to take home. Also a bag of sparkly pencils, erasers, and candies.

When we got home, Jessica and I called Natalie. Her parents took her to Paradise Pizza for lunch. She wore dark glasses so no one could see her eyes. Tomorrow she will wear them to school. Jessica saved a piece of cake for her. I offered to give her my party favors.

*   *   *

Everyone in my family was in a good mood tonight. Even me.

I kept the silver paint on my face and pretended to be a robot to make Alex laugh. Eva and Isabel did not fight at the table. An unprecedented period of world peace. I wonder how long it will last. (Uh-oh. I hear screaming down the hall. The truce has already been broken.)

While we were clearing the table after dinner, my father told me that I have been very mature lately.

So there! I'm mature! I knew it all along! I'm glad my parents have finally caught on.

Will they let me get pierced ears now? Must ask soon. Seize the moment. Grab the second. Arm wrestle the quarter hour.

Earrings are the final frontier. If I could have pierced ears, I would have EVERYTHING I want. Well, almost everything.

Check out what's new with your old friends.